WARNING

This book contains sexually explicit scenes and adult language. It may be considered offensive to some readers. This book is for sale to adults ONLY.

* * * * * * * * * * * * * * * * *

Please store your files wisely where they cannot be accessed by underage readers.

Other Books by Darla Dunbar:

<u>The Romeo Alpha BBW Paranormal Shifter Romance Series</u>

Amanda Walker thinks that she has a normal and boring life. That is until after her 24th birthday. Everything changes when she meets the man who says he was supposed to be her husband. Denying everything the man says, she fights him every step of the way. But after he kidnaps her, Amanda discovers that there are some things about her family that her parents kept a secret all these years. Among the history of the family she learns secrets she thought only happened in story books. Can Amanda tell the difference between truth and lies or is she this mysterious woman that holds the key to a legacy?

<u>Romeo Alpha Blood Lines Romance Series</u>

Twenty-four years have passed in relative peace for Amanda and Romeo. They've raised five children into adulthood and are thoroughly enjoying their lives as the Alpha King and Queen of the werewolves. At twenty-four, Sarina is just stepping into her powers and will be ripe for mating when her birthday comes in two weeks. What no one knows is the danger that lurks just outside their tight knit community. Romeo has made peace with the other clans and has enjoyed that peace, but it will all come crashing down around him when his oldest daughter comes of age to take a mate.

<u>The Alpha Feud BBW Paranormal Shifter Romance Series</u>

Eliza's life consisted of reporting on boring, crowd-pleasing events, like their country livestock fair. With the arrival of two handsome brothers, the lives of Eliza and her best friend, Melissa, are shaken to the core. For Eliza, the arrival of this new man becomes a test of her relationship with her current boyfriend, who she's been happily living with for over six years. Does Hayden, a complete stranger, really wield the power to make Eliza reconsider her relationship with Andrew?

<u>The Alpha Packed BBW Paranormal Shifter Romance Series</u>

Darlene has led a quiet life since suffering through a terrible break-up. She wants nothing more than to spend her time in front of the TV, away from any sort of trouble. But all that goes down the drain when handsome, rugged and rough Idris comes into her life. He is a werewolf on the lookout for his missing pack leader. Darlene quickly finds herself pulled towards this mysterious man and at the same time finds herself falling deeper and deeper into the world of the supernatural.

<u>The Daemon Paranormal Romance Chronicles</u>

The daemon infighting can only be stopped when a strong leader emerges to calm the different factions. Juno appears to be at the heart of the conflict. Things become complicated when Phoebe and Supay try to negotiate with the siren, Juno. The love triangle among Phoebe, Supay and Apollo become tense when Juno's meddling threatens to destroy any romance that develops.

<u>The Mind Talker Paranormal Romance Series</u>

Ananda finds herself on the run and she's not alone. With help from Jared, a stranger that she just met, the two evade capture by an organization that is intent on hunting her kind. Ananda and Jared are able to read minds. When an unfortunate incident happened involving a disturbed individual that resulted in the death of his schoolmates, the secret organization decided to take action.

Get the latest update on new releases from the author at:

https://darladunbar.com/newsletter/

This book is Part Six of "<u>The Leather Satchel</u>
<u>Paranormal Romance Series</u>"

Book 1 - Valtina's Redemption

Valtina is stuck in Middle World, unable to pass on
to The Afterlife. In order to redeem herself from past
deeds done, she must help bring romance back into the
world and stop The Dark Side from destroying love in
its entirety. Following orders issued by Ladaya and
armed with a leather satchel filled with the appropriate
tools and weapons, Valtina must bring romance back
into the lives of Samantha and Joshua, thereby saving
their marriage.

Book 2 - Unfaithful

Amy and Matt's relationship was never meant to be.
The evil forces at work are bent on eliminating love on
Earth. Couples are being mismatched in order to create
chaos. It is Valtina's mission the help Amy find her soul
mate and repair the damage that is being caused by the
dark forces.

Book 3 - Evil Lust

Henry and Claire are meant to be together. But a
succubus has taken over Henry's actions. Under her
spell, Henry has succumbed to lusting after Charlotte,
the human form that the succubus has assumed. If
Claire were to find out, then their marriage will be
ruined beyond repair. It is up to Valtina to break the
succubus' spell and clear Henry's memory of any guilt
that would haunt his love for Claire forever.

Book 4 - Salvaged Soul Mates

The Dark Side is winning. A Mystic has organized the evil monsters to steal every soul on Earth and leave it loveless. It is up to Valtina to do her part to save the human race. Sent by Ladaya back to Earth, Valtina's job is to unite a mismatched couple with their true soul-mates. Sebastian and Claudia were not meant to be married to each other. But a trickster was involved in encouraging the mismatch. Searching through her leather satchel, Valtina found the tools needed to do the job.

Book 5 - Fury of Lust

Valtina's missions are becoming more dangerous and will need the protection of a warrior and emere while out on duty. This time she needs to rid Rachel of a fury and free Sean of his demons. Rachel and Sean are meant to be true lovers but they have been prevented from meeting each other. Valtina must use the arsenal in her leather satchel to ensure that true love follows its course when Rachel and Sean finally meet.

Book 6 - True Lovers

Middle World has been invaded by the wraiths. While the Generals battle the monsters to protect Middle World, Valtina must continue her missions to save love on Earth. The evil forces have brain-washed Penelope and Davis into thinking that their attraction for each other is wrong. Valtina's mission is to clear the way for the couple to see that they were meant for each other and to let true love runs its fateful course.

The Leather Satchel Paranormal Romance Series

True Lovers

Book Six

By Darla Dunbar

Copyright Revelry Publishing 2015

Table of Contents

Chapter One

VALTINA AND Demetri sat silently under the willow tree, anxiously awaiting Ladaya's return. They'd stopped trying to guess how much time had passed since Ladaya returned to The Afterlife; they were now marking the time by the number of wraiths Demetri had slaughtered. So far, the warrior had eliminated five of the monsters. Valtina had known that their sanctuary had been breached, but it hadn't seemed real until she saw the first black hooded creature emerge from the dense grey fog. As time passed, Valtina became more and more nervous; she knew that in this situation, no news was not good news.

Demetri stiffened, and Valtina followed his gaze. Another wraith was approaching from the fog. As the warrior rose to confront the monster, the tip of a silver dagger broke through its chest, and it evaporated where it stood. Ladaya and a spirit Valtina didn't recognize stood before them.

"Ladaya!" Valtina exclaimed, "I was starting to worry!"

"Hello, August." Demetri nodded to the other spirit. August nodded in reply. Demetri continued. "Valtina, this is August, my General. I take it no one is traveling alone now?" he asked, turning to the Generals.

"It's nice to meet you, Valtina. I've heard wonderful things," August began. He turned to Demetri. "No, we've all been instructed to travel with a partner. The wraiths are flooding Middle World, and we believe they're looking for a way in to The Afterlife."

Ladaya watched panic spread over Valtina's face. "Don't worry child," she assured her. "We've learned of a way to defeat them. There's lore of a weapon, a sword forged in the fires of the Underworld that will destroy the wraith army. If the Queen is decapitated with the sword, the entire army will evaporate. They're all connected, you see…" Ladaya trailed off.

"Are we sure the weapon exists?" Demetri asked with an air of doubt. "I mean, lore isn't always reliable."

"We're pretty confident," August answered. "The rest of the lore regarding wraiths has proved true. We have no reason to think the sword is any different."

"So, do you know where it is?" Valtina asked. "Let us help, we can search with the other spirits."

Ladaya smiled. "Once again, I appreciate your offer, and your dedication… but we all have specific jobs to do, and your next mission is the most important to date. Other spirits, whose gifts are suited to the mission, are searching for the sword."

"Ladaya, speaking of weapons…" Valtina began, but was interrupted by her General.

"I know, Valtina," Ladaya sighed. "You want a weapon. As well you should, knowing that Morgonda is targeting you. And at this point, I'd give you a dagger if I could. But I don't believe it would do you much good."

"Why not?" Valtina asked.

"Demetri," Ladaya turned to the warrior, "would you be so kind as to let Valtina hold your dagger for a moment?"

Nodding in confusion, Demetri held his dagger out to Valtina. The moment she touched the weapon, her hand burned in pain. Gasping, she pulled away.

"Ouch!" she cried. "I can't even touch it?!"

"No," Ladaya sighed, "Valtina, your spirit is composed of pure love. The weapon, and its purpose, is in direct conflict with your spirit force, making it impossible for you to hold it."

Valtina was disappointed; she also wished Ladaya had told her that the first time she'd asked for a weapon. It would have saved her a lot of frustration. But the fog continued to grow denser, and Valtina knew that she must stay focused on her mission. "Ok, so I can't protect myself. Where are we going next?" she asked with a slight tone of defeat.

"Las Vegas," Ladaya answered. "We've learned of a dire situation there. I'm sending you to a young woman named Penelope. Her father was a non-denominational minister who worked to help the souls of Sin City. Six years ago, the preacher made a drastic change in his ministry and began preaching vehemently against 'sins of the flesh'. He brainwashed his congregation to believe that even marital sex can bring evil into the home, and should only be indulged in for the purpose of procreation. The result of these ministries has been a sharp decrease in the number of soul-mates pairing up. They believe that their natural sexual attraction goes against God, and that the person they belong with is the person they are LEAST physically attracted to."

"So we're dealing with another evil human?" Valtina asked.

"No," Ladaya answered, "we've received information that the creature currently acting as the minister is actually a shape-shifter. Penelope's real father was killed shortly before the minister began preaching against sex. The spirit of the real minister is trapped in the Underworld; he will be freed when we defeat Morgonda."

Frustration filled Valtina. "SIX years?" she asked. "This has been going on for SIX years, and we're just now doing something about it?"

"Valtina, you must understand," August answered patiently, "Earth is a very big place, and we monitor it the best we can. But Las Vegas has been covered in black fog since I arrived in The Afterlife! And, remember, we can't travel to Earth to determine what kinds of sins and evil are occurring. It wasn't until recently, when we activated you and the other spirits of

Middle World and sent you to Earth, that we became aware of the problem."

"I understand," Valtina answered quietly.

"So, I assume that the shifter is my job?" Demetri asked.

August nodded. "In part. Fatima will meet you at the church. We've assigned other teams to the members of the congregation, and they will also meet you there. We've assigned you, Valtina, to Penelope because we believe she will be the most difficult to repair once the shifter is gone. She lived with the monster; its influence has affected her the most. Also, the shifter replaced Penelope's father before she lost her virginity. Unlike other members of the congregation, who've had and enjoyed sex, Penelope knows nothing of sex except the warped views the shifter placed in her head."

"We aren't taking any chances with the shifter. Demetri, you and the other warriors will combine forces with the emeres, and you will take on the shifter together. Once he's been eliminated, you and Fatima will stay and protect Valtina."

Demetri nodded his understanding. Ladaya turned to Valtina to describe the rest of her mission.

"Penelope's soul-mate is Davis, the son of one of the church deacons. They've known each other since they were small children, and they always got along well. The attraction between them began shortly before the shifter killed Penelope's father. When the minister began preaching against sex, the couple began avoiding each other, ashamed of how they felt in each other's presence. Like Penelope, Davis is a virgin. They will both need your inspiration to trust their natural feelings."

"I can do that," Valtina answered confidently, determined to right the wrongs done by the shape-shifter; she was personally offended by the subject of his ministries.

"Be careful, Valtina," Ladaya reminded her warmly, "and do your best." As Ladaya spoke, the white mist arrived, transporting Valtina and Demetri to Earth.

Chapter Two

Valtina and Demetri were deposited at the front pew of a small, sparsely decorated sanctuary. Fatima stood before them, watching over a slender, brunette woman Valtina knew was Penelope. She blocked the shifter's words as she scanned the rest of the room; two dozen other spirit teams were scattered throughout the congregation.

"You're the last to arrive," Fatima said softy. "Are you ready?" she asked Demetri. The warrior nodded. Fatima signaled the other emeres, and a moment later they rushed in unison to the pulpit. Valtina saw a flash of gold light, and then Demetri and the other warriors attacked as one. Valtina watched as the preacher's features disappeared and were replaced by an opaque, black shadow. The shadow dropped to the ground and remained there, as church members shouted and rushed to their minister's aid. Demetri and Fatima returned to Valtina.

"What are they seeing?" she asked quickly, wondering how they were supposed to inspire the congregation to believe that a man turning into a shadow was completely normal.

"You're seeing the shifter's true form," Demetri explained, "but the emeres put a charm on the congregation; that was the gold light you saw. The church members saw the minister have a heart attack and die at the pulpit. A charm was also placed on the body to retain the minister's appearance until he is buried."

Valtina nodded in understanding and relief. She scanned the room until her powers focused her attention on a lanky, blonde man she instantly recognized as Davis. He gazed longingly at Penelope, consumed with equal desire to comfort her and shame for the other things he wanted to do with her. Valtina felt Penelope should be allowed some time to grieve; the loss of her father was real to her, even if it had actually happened years ago.

"Let's go with Davis for now," Valtina directed. Her partners nodded their agreement. She entered Davis's mind and encouraged him to go home. The spirits rode, unnoticed, in Davis's car and then followed him up to his apartment. The home resembled the church in its simplicity and plainness. A single cross adorned the wall; the living room held outdated furniture, a small television, and shelves of religious books. The most modern object in the apartment was a laptop, which sat on the kitchen counter. Davis sat on the threadbare couch and Valtina entered his mind.

"I hope she's okay… should I check…? The minister would say no. He would tell me to stay away from her, that my thoughts are impure… but what if he was wrong? She makes me feel so good… how could that be evil?" Valtina was pleased to hear that Davis was already questioning the shape-shifter's teachings.

She reached into her leather satchel and retrieved a postcard from a national Christian ministry. She placed the postcard with the pile of mail sitting on Davis's kitchen table and entered his mind once more.

"Oh yes, the mail," he thought to himself. "I should look through that." Davis retrieved the mail and immediately noticed the postcard at the top of the pile. "Hmm…" he found himself thinking, "I wonder what this church says about sex." He turned on his laptop, and was shocked at what he found on the ministry's website. According to their preachers, marital sex was a beautiful thing! The preachers actually *encouraged* its members to maintain healthy sexual relationships with their spouses! Shocked, Davis searched other websites and found similar information. "Why did we never question him?" The thought was his own. "I must go to Penelope." Valtina immediately took the last thought from Davis's mind. "No… she needs space… she's grieving. I'll visit her tomorrow." Valtina was relieved that Davis had been so easy to inspire, but she still had work to do before the two should see each other. She returned to the hallway where Fatima and Demetri waited.

"Let's go check on Penelope," she directed firmly.

The trio arrived at the home Penelope had shared with both her father and the shifter. Valtina quickly entered the young woman's mind, eager to see if the shifter's influence was lifting. Like Davis, Penelope was conflicted by her emotions. Valtina could tell that

Penelope was genuinely saddened by her "father's" death, but at the same time she was beginning to doubt all of his teachings. The main source of this doubt was the overwhelming longing she felt for Davis. He'd been her best friend as a child, and she'd been so angry with herself when she couldn't control her feelings for him. Her father had insisted that those feelings were evil. But if they were, why would she feel so certain that Davis was the only person who could comfort her?

Once again, Valtina rummaged through her trusty leather satchel and retrieved just what she needed to help inspire Penelope. She placed a wedding album and a journal in the minister's closet, and then entered Penelope's mind for the second time. "If only I knew him better… if I could understand what changed him…" Before she even realized where she was going, Penelope arrived at her father's closet. She found her parent's album and her mother's journal… her mother, who she had lost to cancer at the age of five. "Maybe I can learn more about both of them," Penelope thought. She flipped through the album, pleased and shocked by the looks on her parent's faces. The attraction between them was obvious, the looks full of all the feelings Penelope's father had warned her against. She turned to the journal. Her mother had passionately described the couple's wedding night. Penelope didn't have to read any further to know that her father's later teachings had been wrong. Looking through the photographs, she wondered why he had preached what he himself knew to be false. Valtina inspired understanding. "His heart must have broken when mother died. After years without her, he became bitter. He wasn't in his right mind. It wasn't his fault," Penelope thought, a warm peace settling upon her.

"It wasn't his fault… but he was wrong. I'll call Davis tomorrow," Penelope resolved to herself. With that, she returned to her own bedroom and settled in for a surprisingly restful night's sleep.

The next morning, Penelope rose early. Valtina was about to leave Demetri and Fatima with the young woman and check on Davis when Penelope's phone rang. Valtina entered her mind so she could hear both sides of the conversation. She heard Davis's voice.

"I just wanted you to know that I've been thinking about you, and I'm here for you if you need anything," he said. Valtina felt Penelope's heart soar.

"Thank you so much, Davis. The truth is that I could really use a friend right now. Could you meet me for breakfast?"

"Of course."

The couple made plans to meet at a local diner and ended the phone call. Valtina filled Penelope with confidence while she got ready for the day, and then she and her fellow spirit warriors followed Penelope to her car. As they rode in silence, the white mist filled the backseat, where Demetri and Fatima sat.

"Something serious must be happening in Middle World," Demetri called to her. "I'm confident they'll send me back if you're in danger. Good luck!"

When the mist dissipated, Valtina found herself alone. She felt oddly exposed without her fellow soldiers, but knew she had to complete her mission; only then would the mist transport her back to Middle World, where she could find out what was going on. They arrived at the diner, and Valtina followed Penelope through the door. Davis was already sitting at a far booth. He rose as Penelope approached, and then embraced her affectionately.

"I've been so worried about you," Davis said as he released her. "I've already ordered. I hope waffles are still your favorite," he said.

"They are. I can't believe you remembered," Penelope responded, her cheeks blushing.

"I remember everything about you, Penelope," Davis confessed. "I never stopped thinking about you. I've wanted to reach out to you for so long, but I thought it was sinful," he hesitated, afraid to hurt Penelope's feelings. Valtina filled him with encouragement, and he continued. "When I got home from church last night, I started thinking. And then I started reading things online. I think… I think, maybe you father…"

"Was wrong?" Penelope finished the thought.

"You think so too?"

"Yes. I found some of his and mother's things last night. I think he was heartbroken after she died, and that it got worse over time instead of better. I don't think he's been in his right mind," she admitted. Davis reached across the table and took her hand in comfort.

"Penelope, I know this isn't the right time…" Davis was, once again, interrupted.

"I love you, Davis," she blurted out. "I think I've always loved you. I think you're the person I'm supposed to be with. Since Daddy died, I've felt like a fog has lifted. It's like I'm seeing clearly for the first time in years. I love you, and I want to be with you. And I don't think that's sinful… I think God put us together for a reason."

Davis beamed from the other side of the booth. He was filled with a happiness and excitement he'd never experienced before. Valtina heard the question in his head before he spoke it.

"Penelope, this may seem sudden. But I've known I want to be with you for as long as I can remember. Will you marry me?"

Tears welled up from Penelope's eyes and joy rushed through her body. "Yes. I want nothing more than to be your wife, Davis." Davis moved to join his new fiancé on her side of the booth.

"Penelope, I've never been so happy and so sad at the same time. I'm sorry about your father. We don't have to make any announcements until after his service."

"No, I don't want to wait," Penelope insisted. "I feel like I've already lost years with you. I can't wait any longer. Let's go to a chapel, today."

"Today!" Davis cried in excitement. "Today it is." Valtina could have inspired the couple to wait, but she saw no reason to. They were soul-mates, true matches, so why slow down their destiny any longer? Valtina entered Davis's mind and listened as he made reservations for the honeymoon suite at The Royal Vegas Hotel. Then, he began searching through ads for local wedding chapels.

"Nothing with Elvis," Penelope instructed with a laugh. Davis called Viva Lamoure and made a noon appointment.

"Just enough time to get the essentials," Davis smiled as he hung up his phone. "I'll pick you up at 11:30?"

"No! You can't see me before the wedding! I'll meet you at the altar. Don't get to the chapel before 11:45," Penelope said with a smile. The couple kissed sweetly and then parted ways. Confident that they were on the right track, Valtina let them both leave without her. She had preparations to make in the honeymoon suite.

Chapter Three

Valtina arrived at the hotel and found the room to be impeccably clean and gorgeously decorated in modern art and furniture. A heart-shaped Jacuzzi tub sat in one corner of the room in front of the expansive windows. Valtina sat on the king-sized bed and examined the contents of her leather satchel. As always, the perfect items for the mission appeared. Valtina arranged a simple, white silk negligee on the foot of the bed. On the nightstand, she placed a bottle of strawberry lubricant and a satin blindfold. Satisfied that the couple was well-equipped for their first sexual encounter, Valtina left the hotel and headed for the chapel.

Valtina arrived at the chapel at 11:40, just as Penelope got out of a taxi. She wore the dress Valtina recognized from her parents' wedding photos. Valtina entered her mind to see how confident Penelope felt about her impending marriage. To her delight, Valtina found that Penelope would make it down the aisle with no inspiration from her. She watched as Penelope entered the chapel and asked to wait in the bridal room.

Valtina waited anxiously at the chapel entrance. She was eager for the couple to wed and for her mission to be completed. Demetri and Fatima had disappeared hours ago, and neither had returned with an update. Valtina was certain that if the danger was over, someone would be sent to tell her. She'd been on guard for wraiths and other monsters, but so far she'd been safe. But Valtina doubted her luck would last forever. 'It's about time,' she thought to herself at 11:48, when Davis pulled into the chapel's parking lot. Valtina was certain the mist would reappear the moment the couple said "I do." She entered Davis's mind as he walked into the chapel. Like Penelope, Davis was confident about his decision.

'Why am I still here then?' The thought nagged at Valtina. She'd had the same thought on her last mission, as she watched Rachel and Sean make love. Sure, she'd put a bottle of water on the nightstand for them, but the couple could have gotten water for themselves. Valtina hadn't been needed long before the couple had sex, and yet she'd remained for hours of their lovemaking. As Valtina relived her frustrations, the chapel minister appeared and brought her attention back to the task at hand. She had to pay attention; if she WAS still needed, she didn't want to miss anything.

The minister led Davis to the altar and moments later The Wedding March rang out through the chapel speakers. Penelope appeared at the end of the aisle, radiant in her mother's dress. Valtina couldn't help herself; she disappeared into her memories of her own weddings. The memories were even more precious to her now, since she'd learned that in each life, she'd married the same soul, her soul-mate. Their weddings had all been unique and beautiful. Some were small, some were large, but all were filled with the same kind of love present in the chapel with Penelope and Davis.

Valtina gazed back towards the couple just in time to hear the minister pronounce them man and wife. They kissed passionately, their bodies wrapped together. After a few moments, Davis finally pulled away.

"May I escort you to our room?" he asked with a coy smile.

"As fast as you can," Penelope replied with a grin.

Valtina traveled ahead of Penelope and Davis, arriving at the suite long before they did. She grew more and more anxious with each passing moment, and nightmarish thoughts filled her mind. What if the wraiths had succeeded in breaching The Afterlife? What if mist *couldn't* retrieve her, because it no longer existed? Terror filled Valtina at the thought of being left on Earth, alone and defenseless. She felt herself sink into a deep despair and she wondered if there was any point in remaining in the suite. Penelope and Davis were married; there was nothing left for her to do. As she thought about leaving and wondered if there were any safe places left on Earth, Penelope and Davis entered the honeymoon suite. Valtina quickly entered each of their minds in turn; neither was nervous about what lay ahead. In fact, they were both looking forward to it. Valtina was surer than ever that her fellow soldiers had been defeated. Why else would she still be here?

"Davis, did you do this?" Penelope exclaimed, holding up the negligee. Davis's eyes moved from the lingerie to the lubrication and blindfold on the nightstand.

"No, it wasn't me. They must be part of the honeymoon package," Davis concluded with a smile. Observing the couple's happiness, Valtina decided to remain with them for a while longer. Valtina sometimes enjoyed watching the people she was assigned to help experience the purest expression of love.

Davis moved across the room and took his new wife in his arms. "I love you Penelope. I can't wait to show you how much I love you."

Penelope pulled away laughing. "Patience, husband. Let me go change." She smiled and held up the negligee. She darted off to the bathroom; Davis stripped down to his boxer shorts while he waited. A few moments later Penelope returned, looking both seductive and innocent in the white silk lingerie. Davis gasped in amazement at the sight of her.

"Penelope, you look amazing," he said. It took Penelope a few moments to respond. She was distracted by Davis's exposed, well-defined abs and shoulders.

"You look amazing too," she finally replied. She moved across the room and sat next to Davis on the bed. He reached over and tenderly caressed her face, before putting the blindfold over her head to cover her eyes.

"Are you nervous?" he asked.

"No," she answered. She moved in and tenderly took his lower lip into her mouth. She nibbled and teased it, before raising her head slightly and kissing him hungrily. Davis moved his hands up her sides, the soft fabric slightly teasing both of their bodies. He returned her kisses with equal vigor, and gently moved Penelope onto her back. He straddled her, careful to not put any of his weight on her slender body.

"I can't believe we're finally here. I can't believe we waited so long. I love you," he whispered, looking deeply into Penelope's eyes.

"I love you too," she replied, lifting her head to kiss him again. Excitement rushed through Penelope's body as Davis's lips left hers and traced a trail down her body. He stopped for a moment at each of her nipples, sucking and teasing them through the white silk. He continued his journey, pushing the negligee up and exposing Penelope's stomach. She wriggled in anticipation as Davis plunged his face between her legs.

Davis teased her tight pussy with his fingers and tongue; Penelope couldn't tell which part of his body was providing each electrifying sensation, and she stopped trying to figure it out. She let go and gave Davis total control of her body. Soon, Penelope writhed on the bed and cried out in her first release. It took her several moments to catch her breath.

"Baby," she sighed, removing her blindfold. "That was amazing. I had no idea anything could feel so amazing…" Davis positioned himself on top of her and glanced towards the lubrication. Penelope stopped him.

"No, not yet. I want you to feel what I just felt. I want to give you what you just gave me."

She smiled mischievously and rolled her husband onto his back. She tugged at his boxer shorts, revealing his long, thick, throbbing cock. Penelope took him in her hand, gently stroking his soft, silky shaft; she was mesmerized. She positioned herself next to Davis and supported her weight with one elbow. With her other hand, she continued stroking Davis, increasing her speed as she took the tip of his cock into her mouth.

Davis was overwhelmed with sensations. After only a few minutes of Penelope's teasing, he exploded into her mouth. Penelope lapped up every drop hungrily, enjoying the taste of her new husband's juices. She lay beside him, expecting him to need a while to recover from his climax. Although Davis had reached release, his still-hard cock longed for more. He rolled over onto his side, facing Penelope. He pulled her close and pushed his throbbing, aching cock against her stomach.

"Are you ready, baby?" he asked, reaching over his shoulder for the bottle of lube on the nightstand. He wanted to make sure Penelope enjoyed their experience as much as he did.

"Yes baby, so ready," Penelope cried out passionately as Davis teased her with his lube-covered fingers. Instinctively, she lifted one leg, allowing Davis room to enter her. Penelope gasped with pleasure as she felt each inch of her husband's cock slowly push inside her. Once Davis's entire cock was buried within her, the couple lay still for a moment, side by side, and gazed into each other's eyes. They were overwhelmed by the extreme pleasure of being connected. Tentatively, Penelope braced herself with one hand on the headboard and began pushing herself slowly up and down on Davis's cock. She was unable to control her cries as she was consumed with passion for her husband and for the throbbing cock inside of her.

Davis responded to his wife's movements with slow thrusts of his own. He felt at home in Penelope's tight, dripping pussy, and he knew that he was exactly where he belonged. Valtina watched the couple find a beautiful, unbreakable rhythm, and soon they came together, crying out in unison. Davis remained in his wife long after he turned soft; neither wanted to break the connection. They held each other, professed their love, and made plans for their future. The beauty of the scene brought a tear to Valtina's eye; the couple began kissing again and soon resumed their movements against each other. Davis's cock had grown hard again; after a few minutes of thrusting, he moved Penelope flat on her back. As his cock once again disappeared into his wife's welcoming pussy, the white mist returned, and Valtina found herself being carried away.

Chapter Four

"Well done!" Ladaya beamed at Valtina the moment she arrived in Middle World.

"Ladaya, can this be?" Valtina gasped in shock. The grey fog was gone, and Middle World was right again.

"Yes." Ladaya smiled. "One of our soldiers found the sword. Demetri destroyed the wraith Queen several hours ago; the immediate threat is over."

"Demetri killed the Queen?" Valtina asked in surprise.

"Of course. Demetri is the best." Ladaya smiled. "That's why he was assigned to you."

"So what does this mean for us?" Valtina asked. She didn't dare to hope that she'd be sent to The Afterlife. She knew that they'd won the battle, but the war still raged on.

"Morgonda and her other monsters are still pursuing us. There's still a price on your head. But the wraiths were the most populated species working with her. She's suffered a great loss. I'm confident that she'll regroup and come up with a new battle strategy, but for now we are safe."

"So I still have missions to complete?" Valtina asked.

"Yes child, many missions remain. I wish I could give you your ultimate reward, but as you know…"

"I'm powerful. And it's necessary that I be able to return to Earth," Valtina finished. Her General nodded in reply. "But Ladaya, why is it necessary that I remain behind so long? On my last two missions my work was finished long before the mist appeared."

"Your powers, Valtina," Ladaya began. "As I've told you, your spirit force is pure love. Your powers recharge themselves and become stronger when you are in the presence of the truest expression of love. The mist arrives once you're completely recharged," Ladaya explained simply. Valtina smiled in understanding.

"So, sex is my power source?" she laughed.

"Hasn't it always been?" Ladaya smiled.

"What's my next assignment?" Valtina asked hesitantly. She knew that there was work to be done, but she was tired.

"Your next assignment is to stay here and relax for the moment. Now that the wraith army has been destroyed, we must reevaluate and determine our next move. You've worked hard, Valtina, and you've done well. Rest awhile and I will return when I have the details of your next mission," Ladaya smiled and disappeared to The Afterlife.

Valtina found her favorite willow tree and rested beneath its branches. She knew that danger still lay ahead, but for the moment she decided to ignore it. Instead, she turned her attention to the spirits moving around her, looking for someone familiar.

-The End-

If you enjoyed this title, I would appreciate your leaving a review of the book. Good reviews encourage an author to write as well as help books to sell. Good reviews can be just a few short sentences describing what you liked about the book without having a spoiler. If you could spend 30 seconds writing a review, I would appreciate it: you can review this title right now at your favorite retailer.

Here is a preview of **another story** you may also enjoy:

Romeo Alpha: A BBW Paranormal Shifter Romance - Book 1

AMANDA WONDERED how the hell she had gotten so far away from home. When she walked, she usually didn't go past a couple of blocks, but she felt so different today. Something was pushing her further and in a different direction, and she wasn't sure what it was. But she didn't care at the moment, because she just wanted to walk.

Not thinking twice about where she was going, she let her gut instinct give her the direction she needed.

Her grandmother had always told her to go with her gut. She'd said human instinct was better than anything. "Intuition is a girl's best friend," she would say, and then they would both laugh. Talks she and her grandmother had always seemed to pop into her head at the strangest of times, like now.

Here she was, going for a walk, and wondering why she wanted to go in a different direction, and there was her grandmother's voice in her head, propelling her along. Amanda missed her grandmother more with every passing year.

Amanda paused and thought about her life thus far. She had just graduated from college and started working in the local animal hospital, but it wasn't quite like she had thought. She didn't see the care and passion she'd hoped to find in the industry. In the city, being a vet was all about how much money you could make, how many pets you could treat. And, at twenty-four, it was hard to be taken seriously.

Her two female roommates were nice, but they all just went their separate ways. They didn't eat ice cream and watch movies like on *Friends*. They didn't share secrets or even laugh or hang out. They really just slept in the same apartment, and they usually weren't even home at the same time. Except Amanda, that is.

Amanda was always at home, it seemed. She had nowhere else to go, really. The other two girls spent most nights out with their real friends or their boyfriends. Amanda lived a lonely life, but she was happy. At least, she was pretty sure she was happy. After all, she had an upstanding career, and she still had money left over from her savings.

Both her parents had been killed in a car accident years ago. Amanda had graduated from high school with no family there that day or on the day she graduated from college. It was what it was, though, and she knew that her parents watched her from Heaven.

The only positive thing was that her parents had been prepared and had made sure they left enough money and a big enough life insurance policy to help her out. They would be surprised but happy knowing how much that money had helped her in the years after their death. She was proud to say that she was able to live off of it through her college years. She'd never even had to get a job like most kids did. Amanda had been able to focus on her classes.

That freedom wasn't worth it, though. She would have worked three jobs at a time while going to school for one more day with her parents.

However, the account was finally starting to dry up, and she needed to think about what she would do. Sure, she had a new job that could pay her bills, but those loans were piling up with interest. Even a vet job only went so far.

Amanda sighed as she began the trek back toward the house.

Amanda liked her walks in the evening. It helped her to relax, enjoying the quiet time alone. And while Amanda wasn't overweight by any means, it helped slim her waistline, which showed those extra biscuits she liked every now and again.

She turned and began to make her way back to the townhouse she shared with her roommates, but stopped as she heard a noise

A rustling came from behind her, and she turned to see the bushes shaking. Looking over to the other side of the sidewalk, she saw those bushes shake as well. Not wanting to wait around to find out what was behind the leaves, she took off at a run. She swore she heard a growl come from behind her, but she didn't turn to see what was chasing her. That would only slow her down. As she reached the door to her home, she quickly turned the knob and went through headfirst. Shutting the door quickly, she looked out the window. She got a glimpse of a long black furry tail as something ran around to the side of her building.

"What in the world are you doing, Amanda?" Betsy stood there looking at her inquisitively.

"Something was chasing me."

"What?"

"I don't know what it was, but something big and furry was chasing me. I saw a long black tail just now when I walked into the house."

"You mean when you dove into the house?" Betsy's grin faded. "I'll call the game warden. If there is a big animal outside, then none of us need to go out there until they find it and get rid of it."

"Well, I don't want them to kill it."

"I know, silly, but if it's a wild animal, they can take it out to the National Forest and let it loose. The city is no place for a wild animal." Betsy turned and picked up the phone from the receiver.

Amanda stood in shocked silence as she listened to her roommate tell the person on the other end of the phone what had happened.

She knew from Betsy's tone that she and the person on the other end of the phone were questioning her sanity. They lived in a big city, and the closest thing they got to a wild animal was a stray cat or two. They didn't even get raccoons. If there was some huge animal like she thought, then it would make headline news.

Shaking her head in aggravation, Amanda turned toward her room. She suddenly felt silly and didn't want to have to explain what she saw to any more people.

"Amanda? Where are you going? They are on their way and might need to talk to you."

"Tell them it was a dog. Now that I'm thinking about it, it kind of looked like that couple that lives down the road's greyhound. Maybe he just got out."

"Are you sure, Amanda?" Betsy asked, turning and saying something into the phone.

Without saying another word, Amanda shut the door to her room tight and then quickly locked the door. She looked over her room and, seeing the window open and the curtains blowing in the breeze, she ran over to push the window pane down and lock it tight. As she stood there, she looked out into the woods that made up her backyard. There, in the distance, two yellow eyes stared back at her.

Suddenly, more eyes appeared, and it seemed the animals went on forever. She was amazed, since the woods behind her house were very dense and small. The dark night was lit with a full moon. A shiver raced through her as she stood there and stared into the first set of yellow eyes. She quickly shut the curtains and went to sit on her bed. She didn't think she would ever be able to fall asleep knowing what was out there. As she laid her head on the pillow, her mind wondered to large beasts with yellow eyes and sharp fangs. But she was soon fast asleep.

<<◇>>

Amanda awoke with a yawn. It had been almost a month since the incident with what she now called a dog. She had agreed with Betsy that her mind had been playing tricks on her that night. There were often times when she was sure she felt eyes on her, and she would turn in one direction or another, looking. What she was seeking, she didn't know, but somewhere in the back of her mind, she just wanted to know if the eyes she had seen that night had been real or just part of her dreams that evening. She was still so uneasy about it that her walks seemed to get earlier and earlier each evening.

She was just about to walk out the door when her phone started ringing. She quickly grabbed it and pushed the button to answer it.

"Hello."

"Ms. Walker?"

"Yes?"

"Hello, Ms. Walker, my name is Ernest Montgomery. I am calling to tell you that your aunt has passed away."

"My aunt? But I don't have any family. You must have the wrong Ms. Walker."

"No, ma'am. Your father was Joshua Walker, correct? Mother Maureen Walker?"

"Yes."

"Then, I have the right Ms. Walker. It is your father's sister I am referring to. She unexpectedly passed away from a heart attack. I am very sorry for your loss."

"Oh, my gosh! I never knew I even had any family. I am very sad that I didn't get to meet her."

"Yes, ma'am. I'm sure. She was a nice woman. I have also called you to see if you can meet with me. I need to go over her will with you."

"Her will?"

"Yes, ma'am. Your aunt was a wealthy woman."

"Oh? Um, okay. When would you like to meet?"

"The sooner, the better."

"Okay. How about today?"

"That would be great. I am in Slatesville, in the valley. "

"Oh. Okay. That is just forty-five minutes from me. I can be there in a couple of hours."

"Sounds good, ma'am. I am at the *Montgomery Law Firm*. I am the only attorney in the town."

"Okay. Thank you, sir. I will see you soon."

"Yes, ma'am. I'll be waiting."

Amanda fell back on the couch, stunned, for what seemed like forever. Everything was pushed to the back of her mind as she thought about what she had just learned. She had a family. Well, she *did* have a family. Now her aunt was gone. Could there be others in her family who she knew nothing about? She didn't know, but she did know one thing. She wasn't going to find out sitting around here, twiddling her thumbs. She needed to get going fast.

Amanda headed for the kitchen. She wasn't surprised to see that no one was there. Of course her roommates weren't home. They were either in class or with their boyfriends.

Smiling, she made a cup of coffee and drank it slowly, thinking about what she might find out. Then, with a deep sigh, she made her way to her car. She looked at the small Honda with pride. It was a pile of junk to some, but it held a special place in her heart. She hadn't been able to get rid of her father's car. Instead, she had sold her own.

She looked down at the small picture he had taped to the dash near the speedometer. She was about six in the picture, and she had been holding her mom's cheeks in her hands as she kissed her.

She remembered the day like it was yesterday. They had just got to a cabin they vacationed in. She had enjoyed herself so much. The little cabin had one bedroom with a queen-sized bed where her parents slept and a set of bunk beds for her. They had stayed up late roasting marshmallows as her father told her scary stories about wolves and vampires. She had ended up in their bed, snuggled between the two of them. They had spent the next day hiking and walking trails and seeing tons of waterfalls and animals.

She had loved it and had never forgotten. It soon became a family tradition to go camping every year. After some of those trips, they didn't return home.

Instead, they moved on to a different location. The constant moving had been hard on her as a kid, but she would have never told her parents that. She had felt like they were hiding something from her. Of course, she had been young back then and had blown it off as childhood curiosity. Now, with this new family member, she wasn't so sure.

Her parents had been very quiet people. They seemed cautious of everything going on around them and were even a little jumpy at times. Maybe there was more going on here than she thought. She needed to find out.

She wiped away a tear and go in the car. The car had a huge dent in one side and was almost fifteen years old, but it got her where she needed to go. She slid the car into drive and smiled to herself.

"Dad would be proud that his car was still running so good, wouldn't he, Trixy?" She and her father had named the car together.

Amanda turned onto the next road and made her way down the narrow two-lane road that led into the mountains. She had never been this way because her parents always went the long way around the mountains. They said they liked to take the scenic route.

She came to a small wooden sign that said *Slatesville—Welcome to your home away from home.* She smiled at the welcoming sign and kept on her way to the town. As she drove, she was amazed at how beautiful everything was. The low-hanging branches of the trees scraped the roof of the car every once in a while.

She was amazed at how many animals she saw. Deer acted as if they weren't afraid of her car. Raccoons were plentiful, and she jumped when a large black snake slithered across the road. There were people all around, and they watched her car curiously as she made her way down the street.

The town reminded her of a long lost western ghost town. It was a little spooky, and she caught herself checking the doors to make sure they were locked. The men nodded at her as she moved forward and many of the people smiled, although they held themselves back a little.

Amanda finally saw the sign that said *Montgomery Law Firm*. She pulled into one of the many vacant parking spots and slowly got out of the car. A handsome man leaned against the building she was about to enter. His brown eyes had flecks of yellow and orange in their deep depths. She smiled slightly, and the man just continued to stare as he looked her over slowly.

"Can I help you, ma'am?"

"I am just here to see Mr. Montgomery."

"Well, you're in the right place, Miss…?"

"Oh, Amanda. Amanda Walker. And you are?"

Something changed in his eyes as he smiled at her and made his way to her side. He held out his hand to her. "Name's Curtis Livingston."

"Oh. Do you live here?"

"Yes. I'm one of the controlling partners here in Slatesville. Well, I have to be going. It was good to meet you."

"You, too, Mr. Livingston."

"Please, call me Curt. Everyone does."

"Only if you call me Amanda."

"That's a deal, sweet lady." She flushed all over when he raised her hand to his lips and gently caressed her knuckles with a brief touch of his mouth. She felt the rise in temperature in her cheeks spread across her upper chest. She stood there and watched as he walked away from her down the street to slip inside a store. She felt foolish and realized that she had been staring. She shook her head, trying to think straight and clear the thoughts that were running through her mind.

Amanda was always aware that she wasn't the Barbie doll type of girl. Although she wasn't fat, she wasn't rail thin, which most men liked, either. Her waist and stomach didn't look like a washboard, although it didn't look like a bunch of bread dough either.

She instantly felt inadequate and quickly turned around to walk to the door of the attorney's office. Knocking, she was surprised when the door instantly opened. The man who opened the door wasn't what she expected. Mr. Montgomery was a short, pudgy man. He didn't wear a business suit, and he didn't seem stuffy at all. He was older and had a short goatee around his mouth. His hair was pulled back into a ponytail at the back of his neck, and he smiled when he saw her.

"You must be Amanda. You look just like your father, except for your eyes. You have your mother's eyes. Let's hope you didn't inherit your father's temper, though," he chuckled.

"You knew my father?"

"Oh, why yes, my dear. We grew up together, Josh and I. Have to say we got into a lot of trouble as kids, and your aunt Mabel was always there to wag her finger and tell on us. You see, there were the three of us; Joshua, Jeremiah, and I. We were called the three musketeers. Mabel wanted to be the fourth, but you know boys. We would never let her, so she always ran and told on us to get back at us for not including her; the little minx." He told the story fondly, and she instantly knew that this man held her family in the highest regard. She also knew he was her ticket to finding out the truth about her family.

"Do I have any more family that I don't know of?" She held her breath, as though she were a child again, asking if Santa Claus was real.

"I am sure you do, my dear. Unfortunately, your aunt was the last of your father's line. She couldn't have any children, and most of the family was killed in a fire in '90. I am sure there is still family on your mother's side, though. However, I must warn you that they are not the kind of people you want to know. Now, if you will come in, I will tell you about everything that now belongs to you."

"What?"

"Oh, my dear, you must know that your father's family had a legacy. You are the only Traverse left to take over the family business."

"What? I don't know what you're talking about."

"They never did tell you who you really are, did they? Oh, you poor child. I am afraid you are going to learn some things about yourself that are going to be hard for you. You must still be a virgin as well."

"I beg your pardon, sir, but I don't see how that's any of your damn business."

"No, my dear, I do not mean to be crude. I was just saying that you have never undergone the Change. It will happen, though. You recently turned twenty-four, and everything changes now."

"What change? What in the hell are you talking about?"

"They hid that from you, too? Oh my gosh. You don't know? Oh, Lord. Okay, first things first. You are now the owner of your family's estate."

"Family estate? So I have a house."

He smiled kindly at her. "Not just a house, my dear. It is what holds the legacy of your family name together. The estate has fifteen bedrooms with their own bathrooms and fireplaces, a kitchen, dining room, parlor, living area, office, library, Carolina room, staff quarters, wrap-around porch with two different sections screened in, pool, tennis courts and 300 acres. It was the pride and joy of your ancestor, Edgar. He was a distant grandfather of yours."

"Oh my gosh."

"Yes, ma'am. How about this? How about I get the keys and directions to the place? You go take a look at it, and then we can talk tomorrow about what you want to do. Stephan has been looking over things, and since your aunt's death, he has given everyone time off until you arrive and decide where to go from there."

Amanda wasn't sure she had the energy to deal with all of this tonight. "Unfortunately, it is very late. Is there somewhere that I can stay for a couple days and then I can go from there and take the day tomorrow to go look at the place?"

"That is perfect. Just give me a second, and I'll find a place for you to stay tonight."

Amanda sat quietly and listened to him talk on his phone. She didn't even hear his words as she thought of what she was going to do.

"I have gotten you a little cabin to rent down the road," he said, drawing her attention back to him. "It is in the woods a little but has electricity and such. On such short notice, I couldn't find anything else. It is only about ten minutes away. The key will be under the mat at the front door. Just go on in and make yourself at home."

"That is perfect. Thank you so much."

"You're welcome, my dear, and we will talk tomorrow. Say ten o'clock tomorrow morning? We will meet here and go to see the house together."

"Perfect. Thank you, Mr. Montgomery."

If you enjoyed this sample then look for **Romeo Alpha: A BBW Paranormal Shifter Romance - Book 1.**

Here is a preview of **another story** you may also enjoy:

The Beginning - The Daemon Paranormal Romance Chronicles, Book 6

THE CALL of an archer could be heard on the battlement. Juno snorted. It wasn't really by choice that she was here with the Romans. Unlike other daemons, she had no allegiance. Although the majority of sirens were part of the Greek tribe of daemons, sirens were not creatures that claimed allegiance to everything. She had, unfortunately, ended up here because of outside circumstances.

Not long ago, she had created a careful plan to wreck the life of Phoebe Williams. At the time, she had hoped that it would bring Supay back to her. That had never materialized and she had instead been left with Apollo. Like her, he had been left without a daemon tribe. After her last attempt at breaking Supay and Phoebe apart, Apollo had been left to suffer from the fall out. He had hoped that Phoebe would choose him in the end. When she had not, he had thrown all of his efforts behind the Roman tribe. They were a rough and tumble bunch, but he no longer seemed to care. Instead, Apollo had quickly developed a singular focus on revenge. Juno had thrown her lot in with Apollo out of the hope that something would jar Supay out of his sickeningly complacent relationship with Phoebe.

Gazing back at the archers, Juno just shook her head. The slight tilt of her chin caused her straight black hair to sway back and forth. Her overly large eyes narrowed uncharacteristically as she tried to hide her annoyance at the Romans. For some reason, they seemed to think that this daemon war was a medieval battlefield. Over the last few months, they had started building supplies and weapons at this lonely base in Sicily. Since she had sworn to stay out of the fight due to her agreement with Phoebe, Juno could not step in and show them how they were doing it wrong. For starters, they had placed the archers on the lowest wall. As the easiest location to climb, the lowest wall would be better suited to giant vats of tar and boulders. Other than a complete lack of knowledge in this field, the Romans also lacked the ability to see that they would be easily routed. Although modern weapons and techniques drew more public attention to the daemon wars, they were also more effective.

Sniffing disdainfully, Juno went back into the castle. She may have promised not to actively fight, but that didn't mean that she could not remain up-to-date on the latest happenings in the daemon world. Purposefully navigating the corridors of the castle, she began to climb the narrow stairs that led to the north tower. With its poorly made steps and drafty interior, few people bothered to enter this part of the castle. This one fact made it perfect for her use.

Entering the tower, Juno set about closing the curtains. At the last curtain, she stopped and peered out at the ground. Below her, Apollo was shouting orders as he tried to get the troops in line. As she watched him, Juno felt a stirring of something within her heart. Not long ago, she had convinced Apollo to sleep with her. Although he had been appalled at the idea when she asked, he had readily returned to her bed since that time. Juno sighed. The life of a siren was never easy. Long ago, she had planned out a different, beautiful life for herself. Since that time, everything had gone wrong and now she was just another siren operating in a chaotic world.

Approaching the sink, she filled several pitchers with water. Each time one pitcher filled, she brought it to the table and used it to fill up a scrying basin. Circular and sleek, the ebony marble gleamed in the evening light. In just a few moments, she would use it to gaze across the world to watch the enemy at work.

Sitting at the table, Juno began to focus her mind. The clutter of her thoughts would not quiet readily, so she leaned back with a sigh. If she could not watch the Greeks mount an attack or Supay attempt to stop the battle, she should do something else. Her mind wandered as she thought about what she needed. After all this time, she had allotted very few moments to herself. Her rosebud lips pursed slightly before relaxing into a grin. Yes, this was just the time for her to revisit her past. A reminder of how she arrived at this place in life would be just the thing that she needed to renew her focus. Settling into the chair further, she waved her hand confidently across the water of the scrying tub. As the ripples expanded outward, pictures began to reveal themselves.

Across the field, a young, beautiful girl darted among the sheep. The dappled sunlight on the ground jostled merrily as the leaves moved in time with each gust of the breeze. Gorgeous and strangely innocent, the young girl fell next to the herd of sheep after a stray rock tripped her up. Laughing prettily, she shook out her straight black hair from a messy bun. The raven black hair fell neatly on her back as she gently combed her fingers through it. Gazing out at the sheep, young Juno knew that there were few better places to be in the world.

Each morning, she picked up her crook and a loaf of bread before heading out toward the Andes. Over recent years, her tribe of sirens had settled down in the area. Known for causing trouble, they never stayed anywhere for more than five or ten years. This time, Juno wanted them to stay. She loved waking up to the smell of coffee brewing and wandering the fields with her sheep. Her mother, Circe, had given her this task to keep her out of trouble. Until her nineteenth birthday, Juno was an untrained siren. Unfamiliar with the ways of the world or sirens, she was told to keep herself out of mischief. As a shepherdess, it would be next to impossible to get into trouble. Honestly, Juno preferred her life this way. None of the sirens like her Aunt Pasiphae or her mother were ever happy. They pretended to be happy and were certainly charming, but the siren way of life tended to be a lonely one. Men were taken and used, but never kept, and love was forbidden. According to her mother, it was impossible for a siren to ever become anything else.

Leaning back into the sweet meadow grass, Juno relaxed luxuriously on her arms. The noonday sun beat above her head and reminded her that it was time for lunch. Rolling over, she reached for her pack and pulled out the loaf of bread. It would be eaten with a small jug of milk. She sighed and her dainty eyelashes drooped slightly. The jug of milk was leaking again. Today would be another day that she would go home starving.

Just as Juno was about to begin her lunch, she heard a noise at the far end of the meadow. Some of her sheep were darting out of the way, as strange sheep approached. Standing up quickly, Juno dropped the loaf of bread on the ground. Cursing at her stupidity, she leaned down to pick it up. With her intent focus on cleaning the bread, she almost forgot about the strange sheep. She glanced up just in time to see a large, black dog dart into view. It seemed intent on herding the sheep into the meadow until it caught sight of her. The sudden shock of seeing someone else caused the dog to lose focus. Before Juno's eyes, the black canine transformed into the naked form of a young man.

Her almond eyes opened widely. "Sir...?" she asked curiously.

Groaning in embarrassment, the young man reached around for something to cover himself with. Juno realized his shame and smiled. Unwrapping the shawl around her waist, she tossed it over to him. Grinning bashfully, the young man tied it around his waist and walked over.

He reached out his hand. "Hi, I'm Supay. I... well. I apologize. This doesn't normally happen. Surprises still jolt me out of shape shifting. I'm still learning. What's your name?"

Juno smiled prettily and stretched out her thin, delicate hand. "I'm Juno. Don't worry about your mistake. I think you're the first person I've seen up here in months and the first man I've seen at all in years."

Supay tilted his head. "What do you mean? How could you not see a man for years?"

If you enjoyed this sample then look for **The Beginning - The Daemon Paranormal Romance Chronicles, Book 6**.

Other Books by Darla Dunbar

- The Romeo Alpha BBW Paranormal Shifter Romance Series

- Romeo Alpha Blood Lines Romance Series

- The Alpha Feud BBW Paranormal Shifter Romance Series

- The Alpha Packed BBW Paranormal Shifter Romance Series

- The Daemon Paranormal Romance Chronicles

- The Mind Talker Paranormal Romance Series

Get the latest update on new releases from the author at:

https://darladunbar.com/newsletter/

About the Author - Darla Dunbar

Darla has been interested in paranormal romance since she was a teenager in high school. It was then that she discovered she could fulfill her fantasies through her writing.

Observing people and human behavior in the area of romance has always been one of her favorite pastimes. Combining that with an overactive imagination is a sure fire way of coming up with interesting themes.

Connect with Darla Dunbar

I really appreciate you reading my book! Here are my social media coordinates:

Friend me on Facebook:
https://www.facebook.com/darladunbar/

Follow me on Twitter: https://twitter.com/DarlDunbar

Check me out on Goodreads:
https://www.goodreads.com/author/show/8425857.Darl
a_Dunbar

Subscribe to my newsletter:
https://darladunbar.com/newsletter/

Visit my website: https://darladunbar.com/

www.ingramcontent.com/pod-product-compliance
Lightning Source LLC
Chambersburg PA
CBHW031631200726
48288CB00019B/1375